Buster Bunny in
THE GREAT
HOMEWORK CHASE

This Tiny Toon Adventures Book is published by Longmeadow Press, in association with Sammis Publishing.
Distributed by Book Sales, Inc., 110 Enterprise Ave., Secaucus, NJ 07904

With special thanks to
Guy Gilchrist • Jim Bresnahan • Tom Brenner • Mary Gilchrist
John Cacanindin • Ron Venancio • Rich Montasanto
Allan Mogel • Gary A. Lewis

Printed in the United States of America
0 9 8 7 6 5 4 3 2 1

Buster Bunny in
THE GREAT
HOMEWORK CHASE

written by Gary A. Lewis

Illustrated by
The Guy Gilchrist Studios

Buster Bunny finished reading his homework and rubbed his eyes. It was late at night and a cool breeze drifted in through his open door. Buster yawned and stretched. The homework was for Wisecracks 101, the course he took with Professor Bugs Bunny at Acme Looniversity. Buster was doing well in the course, but homework was still important. He was really glad he had finished.

The breeze from outside got stronger, gently rustling his paper. Then— before Buster could blink, the wind picked up his homework and whisked it out the open door.

5

For a second, Buster just stared. MY HOMEWORK! a voice inside him shrieked. Then, with a squeal, he jumped up—just in time to see his homework flying merrily down the block.

"MY HOMEWORK!" he shrieked out loud.

It took Buster Bunny five seconds to reach the sidewalk. He took off after his homework just as it blew across the street. Then it blew right into the window of a passing car.

"MY HOMEWORK!" Buster cried to the driver, racing to keep up. But the driver couldn't hear him.

Buster, along with three dogs, chased the car until it stopped at the next traffic light. But just as he reached the car, his homework flew out the opposite window and up into the branches of a tree.

"MY HOMEWORK!" Buster yelled.

Plucky Duck happened to pass by at that moment.

"Hey, Buster old buddy!" he said. "Did you finish your homework yet?"

"MY HOMEWORK!" Buster yelled, starting to climb the tree. "It's up there!"

"I'll give you a boost," said Plucky.

Buster had almost reached the top of the tree when a big, black crow flew past him. It picked up Buster's homework and flew away.

Buster and Plucky chased the crow all the way out into the country. The crow finally came to rest on a big scarecrow in the middle of a field.

15

Hamton was riding his bicycle down the road when he saw Buster and Plucky trying to sneak up on the crow.

"Hey, what are you guys doing?" he called. But that frightened the crow. The crow opened its beak to let out a squawk. Buster's homework went flying again.

"Oh, no," groaned Buster. "MY HOMEWORK!"

Buster, Plucky, and Hamton raced after the homework. It flew up and around the farm. It finally came to rest on a horn of a big old bull who was standing in a field.

"MY HOMEWORK!" Buster shouted.

"Now what are we going to do?" Plucky asked.

"We've got to help Buster," said Hamton. "You go in there and get his homework."

"Not me," said Plucky. "You go."

Buster slowly opened the gate and walked toward the bull. He just had to get his homework back.

The bull stamped his foot and shook his head. Buster's homework flew off the horn and into the air again.

"MY HOMEWORK!" cried Buster, taking off after it. Plucky and Hamton ran after him.

Buster's homework flew down the road. Then it took a right at the crossroad and floated over the river.

"MY HOMEWORK!" Buster yelled.

"There's a boat!" said Plucky.

"Let's go!" added Hamton.

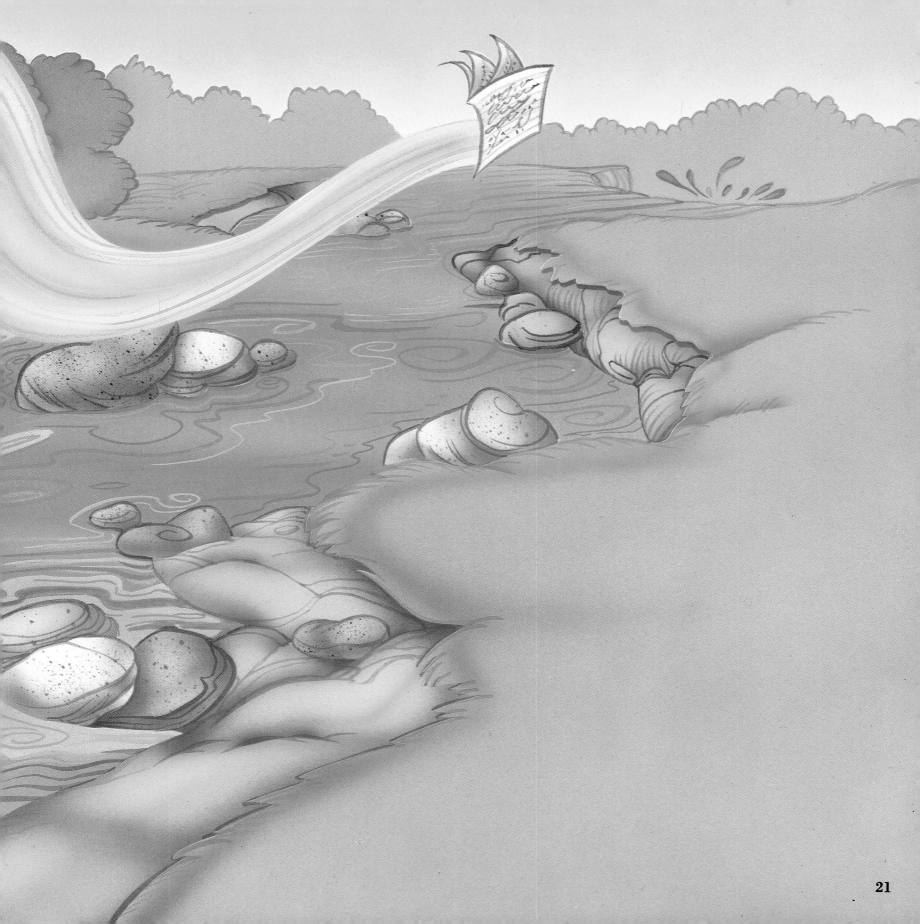

The rowboat and Buster's homework went over the falls at the same time.

But before Buster could grab it, his homework floated gently down…and right into the river.

"MY HOMEWORK!" moaned Buster. "What am I going to do?"

"…and that's what happened to my homework," Buster told Professor Bunny, when everyone else was handing their homework in.

"I'm sorry, Buster," Professor Bunny shook his head, "but I'm going to have to give you a failing grade. And that means you'll be flunking out of Acme Looniversity."

"What?" said Buster. "That can't be!"

"I'm afraid it is," said Professor Bunny.

Buster dragged himself out of class. He ended up on the steps in front of Acme Loo. He sat there, his head in his hands. His life was over. He would move to another town, far, far, away. Perhaps someone would give him a job....

Someone was shaking his shoulder. "Buster! Buster!" a familiar voice said. It sounded like Babs.

"Leave me alone," muttered Buster. "I don't want to talk to you. I don't want to talk to anyone."

But Babs kept shaking his shoulder.

25

"Just leave me a —huh?" Buster Bunny picked up his head and looked around. He was sitting in his room at his desk, with his homework in front of him. Sunlight streamed through the window.

"Buster?" Babs said again, shaking him. "Wake up. You must've fallen asleep here last night."

Buster rubbed his eyes. "You mean it was all a dream?" he said.

"What was all a dream?" asked Babs.

But Buster didn't answer. He had just noticed the clock. It said ten minutes to ten! Wisecracks 101 ended at 10 o'clock sharp. He had to get his homework to Professor Bunny in ten minutes!

"MY HOMEWORK!" Buster yelled. In a flash, he grabbed the homework and leaped for the door.

27

"Buster! Where are you going?" Babs said, popping up the hole after him. "We're supposed to—"

"I can't talk now!" Buster shouted back at her. "I have to get my homework to Professor Bunny. It's ten minutes to ten, and class ends at ten o'clock!"

"But Buster!" Babs shouted back. "Class isn't —" But Buster couldn't hear her.

Buster raced for Acme Looniversity. He just had to get the homework in on time.

He reached Acme Looniversity with one minute to spare. He tried to open the front door, but it wouldn't budge.

"It's locked! It's locked!" he cried, rattling the door. "Somebody let me in. My homework's going to be late!"

"Buster! Listen!" said Babs, finally catching up with him. "Of course the door is locked. Your homework isn't due today. It's due tomorrow! Today is Sunday. School's closed."

"Oh," said Buster, sitting down hard on the steps. He stared up at Babs, and then down at the homework. And then he started to laugh. He laughed so hard that Babs couldn't help but join in.

And after Buster told Babs all about his dream, she laughed even harder.